ALICE WALKER

Paintings by

CATHERINE DEETER

FINDING THE GREEN STONE

HARCOURT BRACE & COMPANY

San Diego   New York   London

Requests for permission to make copies of any part of the work
should be mailed to: Permissions Department,
Harcourt Brace & Company,
6277 Sea Harbor Drive, Orlando, Florida 32887-6777.

Library of Congress Cataloging-in-Publication Data
Walker, Alice, 1944–
    Finding the green stone/by Alice Walker; illustrated by
Catherine Deeter.
      p.   cm.
      Summary: After saying unkind things to family and friends, Johnny
loses both his green stone and his interest in life, and he only
recovers them when he discovers love in his heart.
ISBN 0-15-227538-X
[1. Conduct of life—Fiction.   2. Afro-Americans—Fiction.]
I. Deeter Catherine ill.   II. Title.
PZ7.W15213Fi   1991
[E]—dc20   90-33038

Printed in Hong Kong

J I H G F

The illustrations in this book were done in acrylic on Strathmore illustration board.
The text and display type were set in Brighton Light by Thompson Type, San Diego, California.
Color separations by Bright Arts Ltd., Singapore
Printed by South China Printing Co. Ltd., Hong Kong
This book was printed on totally chlorine-free Nymolla Matte Art paper.
Production supervision by Warren Wallerstein and Rebecca Miller Garcia

To all children
everywhere
&
to the eternal
child
within myself
& you.
—A. W.

For my parents, Irv and Marie Deeter
—C. D.

Right at this very time, in a small community on the Earth, live a brother and sister who have identical, iridescent green stones. The stones shine brightly and are small enough to fit into their hands. The children prize their stones and often play with them, taking them out of their pockets and holding them up to the sun, putting them in the clear water of the seaside among the rocks and plucking them out again, and so on. They are very happy with their stones.

But one day Johnny, the brother, lost his green stone. He looked everywhere for it.

Then he looked at his sister Katie's green stone, and, because his own stone was missing, he imagined that hers looked bigger and shinier than ever. He thought maybe his green stone had disappeared into hers.

"You've stolen my green stone!" he said.

"No way!" said Katie.

Johnny frowned at her and tried to grab her green stone — and even the memory of his own stone vanished.

As the days passed, Johnny became very dull and sat for hours under the big tree in the center of the community.

But Katie never forgot that Johnny had once possessed his very own brightly glowing green stone, exactly like hers. And every day, while he sat under the tree fuming and casting mean looks at everybody who passed and sometimes muttering nasty things as well, she brought him her green stone to hold and reminded him that he had once had one too.

At first, Johnny liked to play with Katie's stone, because whenever he did so he felt much better. But then he would remember that it was hers and that he did not have one of his own, and he would become angry.

One day, when Johnny was feeling this way, he tried to steal Katie's stone by pretending it was his.

"This is my green stone," he cried, clutching it in his fist, not intending to give it back, "not yours!"

But as soon as he did that, the stone turned gray in his hand, just like the rocks by the ocean, and when he looked over at Katie again she had her green stone, as bright and shining as ever!

Johnny felt sad. He realized that stealing somebody else's green stone would never make it his. Besides, it was lonely under the big tree, and trying to look mean all day was boring.

One day he mustered the courage to talk about his change of heart to Katie,
who rarely talked to him now because she was afraid.

"I will never try to steal your green stone again," he said to her. "But I miss my
own stone *so* much. Will you help me find it?"

At first Katie didn't know what to do. How could she believe Johnny meant
what he said? That he would not try to grab her green stone?

"No," she said, after a long pause. "I can't help you at all."

Johnny's eyes were bright with unshed tears. Katie could see he meant her no
harm, but something inside her liked being the powerful one for a change.

"No," she said again, sticking out her chest just as she'd seen Johnny do.
But when she said "No" the second time, with a new coldness in her heart,
her own green stone began to flicker and almost stopped shining!

Katie glanced at Johnny's sweet, sad face, so like her own, and then at her
flickering green stone. Being spiteful to her brother would never work.

"I love you, Johnny," she said quietly. "I'm happiest when you have your very
own green stone. I will do everything I can to help you find it."

The radiance of her stone, when she said this and reached for Johnny's hand,
dazzled them both.

Johnny and Katie set out on their search, hearts pounding, hand in hand.

They looked first near Old Mr. Rose-harp's house.

"I'm afraid to go up to the porch," said Johnny. "Last week, when Mr. Roseharp came by the big tree on his way to the store, I called him a bad name."

But old Mr. Roseharp had seen them coming and stood on his porch in his long red nightshirt, a big yellow broom in his hand. He lived alone in a little wooden house painted blue, and all over it there were painted flowers. In some places you almost couldn't tell where his flower garden ended and his house began.

Old Mr. Roseharp looked down at Johnny and Katie expectantly.

Katie gave Johnny a nudge in the ribs to help him speak up. She could see that Mr. Roseharp was more sad than angry because of what Johnny had said.

"Since I called you a bad name," said Johnny, "I lost my green stone."

"Oh, no!" said old Mr. Roseharp, who knew what a tragedy that was.

He immediately tucked his nightshirt into his pants and put down his broom. Shaking his head with concern and saying, "Uh, uh, uh," he came down to where Katie and Johnny stood and began, right there in his own yard, to help them look.

Next they went to the woods where Johnny and Katie's father was busy loading a big pulpwood truck, using a noisy machine to lift the cut-up pieces of the trees. He turned it off when he saw them coming.

Again Johnny hung back, and this time he kicked at the ground with his toe.

"What's the matter?" asked Katie.

"Last week I told Daddy I was ashamed of him for being the driver of a stupid pulpwood truck. I hurt his feelings and I don't know how to tell him I'm sorry."

But Johnny's father, Mr. Oaks, looked into Johnny's eyes and saw how sad they were.

"What's wrong, son?" he asked gently, folding Johnny in his large arms.

For some reason, being held in his father's arms made Johnny cry and cry. "I'm so sorry for what I said about you driving the pulpwood truck," he said through his tears. "I know it's the only way you can make a living. The only way you can help Mama feed and clothe us all."

"Hey, I knew you didn't mean it," said his father. "I knew you only said it because you hate what pulpwooding does to the trees. I hate it, too."

"And since I said it," said Johnny, "I've lost my green stone."

Mr. Oaks whistled in dismay. He'd lost his own stone many times in his life and each time he had felt terrible. He hugged Johnny and kissed him firmly on the forehead.

When Johnny and Katie and old Mr. Roseharp turned away, Mr. Oaks followed them in his truck.

Mr. Oaks wore his stone on a thong around his neck, Katie had made an earring of hers, and old Mr. Roseharp wore his on his hat. As they moved along, the stones sparkled and shone.

Soon Katie and Johnny saw their mother coming. Since she was the only doctor in their little community, she was always dressed for work and moving very fast. She was wearing a white pantsuit and carrying her black doctor's bag. Her green stone was an especially beautiful one, and because she was always in a hurry and changed clothes so often, she carried it, for safekeeping, in her cheek, which made her look like a mother squirrel carrying a large nut. When she saw everyone coming she took it out of her cheek and closed her hand around it. It shone so brightly that her fist seemed to have a green light in it.

"What's the matter? What's the matter?" their mother asked, kissing Mr. Oaks and Katie and Johnny. She stood tapping her foot as she waited for their reply.

Both Katie and Johnny wondered if they should tell her. Their mother was always in such a hurry that telling her things of importance sometimes felt like throwing your heart against the wind. She would cluck over you for about a minute, then she'd run off to tend to somebody who really needed attention.

Johnny had complained to her about this just last week. How she was never around like the other children's mothers and how he never got hugs and cookies and milk when he came home from school. He wanted another mother entirely from the one he had, he had said.

Still, with Katie's warm little fingers urging him on, Johnny said:

"It's nothing much." He thought: She's probably on her way to deliver a baby, for heaven's sake! "It's just that I lost my green stone."

"You what?" said his mother, dropping her bag — something he'd never seen her do.

Johnny thought that his mother knew almost everything, even if she was usually too busy to say so.

"Do you know where it might be?" he asked. "Do you have it?"

"I can't keep up with every single thing, Johnny," said his mother, in a voice that sounded like she was tired of trying. "Maybe if you'd do a better job of cleaning up your room you wouldn't need help finding your stuff. And no, I do not have your green stone. I have my own."

She picked up her bag, looked at her watch, and placed her own green stone back in her cheek. It tasted like copper. She spat it out and looked at it. It was like a small, sickly olive.

"Oh-oh," she said.

Then she put her arm around Johnny's shoulder. "Listen, son, everybody has his or her own green stone. You ought to know that by now. Nobody can give it to you and nobody can take it away. Only you can misplace or lose it. If you've lost it, it's your own fault."

Johnny felt sadder than he'd ever felt in his life. He thought about his beautiful green stone and how he would probably never see it again. And about how his mother, whom he loved and would never wish to replace with another, always spoke so impatiently. He knew she would not have time to help them look. Without his mother's help, they had no chance at all, Johnny felt.

To his surprise, however, his mother took his hand and said, in her fast, leaping-over-the-gatepost voice: "We will get everybody in the community to help look for your green stone anyway!" She smiled over at Mr. Oaks, as if seeing him for the first time, even though she'd already kissed him, and he smiled back at her. And they all set off down the road.

Before Johnny knew it, he and Katie, Mr. and Dr. Oaks, and old Mr. Roseharp were being followed by Miss Rivers, Johnny and Katie's teacher, Mr. Skies, the minister, and Mr. Birdfield, the shoeshine man. Sunny, the paperboy, and all their classmates and friends also came along. There was even a baby crawling after them. Its glowing green stone was the handle of its pacifier. The dog that was its guardian walked beside it, a green stone glistening in its collar.

Johnny felt embarrassed that all these people knew he had lost his green stone, but Katie went back and picked up the baby, who was almost as large as she was, and then held on to her brother's hand. Johnny looked at his sister's hopeful face, and at the baby who seemed so happy to be out strolling with the big people, and tried to keep his chin up for their sakes.

Finally, after hours and hours of searching — under doorsteps, in orchards, in flowerbeds, and even on the cliff — everyone was tired and so they stopped to rest under the big tree. The tree's green stone was one of its millions of fat green leaves. Sometimes it was hard to see, but not today. Today it sparkled brightly, way up high above everybody's head, and this made Johnny sadder still.

Tears came again to his eyes. He was not crying just because he'd lost the green stone; he knew that because of his hurtful behavior, he deserved to lose it. He was crying because all these people, and especially Katie, loved him and were trying to help him find his green stone, even though they knew perfectly well he could only find it for himself!

Idly, Johnny picked up a small rock and fondled it.

He was puzzled that everyone in his community wanted to help him do something he could only do himself, and in his puzzlement, he began to feel as if a giant bee were buzzing in his chest. It felt exactly as if all the warmth inside himself was trying to rush out to people around him. He noticed that as soon as the warmth that was inside him touched them, they began to shine.

"You should all go home," he said to Katie, ashamed to have taken up so much of everyone's time. "You've wasted a whole afternoon. There's no point in helping me look for something that you can't actually help me find."

"We wanted to be with you when you found it!" said Katie, softly, wiping Johnny's tears away with her sleeve.

And sure enough, when Johnny followed Katie's gaze and looked down at his hand, what did he see? Not the dull and lifeless rock that he'd thought he was holding, but his very own bright green stone!

Johnny jumped up and began to dance around the tree. And all the people —
his mother and father, old Mr. Roseharp, his teacher and minister and the
shoeshine man and the paper boy, and Katie — returned the smile he gave them.

They welcomed the rising of a bright green sun in his heart, which they knew was Johnny's love for them, its warm light overflowing the small brown fingers clutched close to his chest.